The Adventures
Of
Paul Sparrow

The Adventures
Of
Paul Sparrow

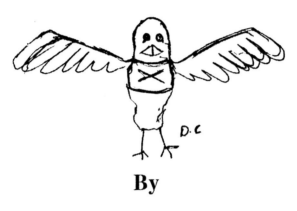

By

Constance Haughton

iUniverse, Inc.
New York Lincoln Shanghai

The Adventures Of Paul Sparrow

iUniverse books may be ordered through booksellers or by contacting:

iUniverse
2021 Pine Lake Road, Suite 100
Lincoln, NE 68512
www.iuniverse.com
1-800-Authors (1-800-288-4677)

Illustrations are by Daniel, Adam and Peter Collins.

ISBN-13: 978-0-595-38147-0 (pbk)
ISBN-13: 978-0-595-82515-8 (ebk)
ISBN-10: 0-595-38147-2 (pbk)
ISBN-10: 0-595-82515-X (ebk)

Printed in the United States of America

Contents

Preface

These stories took shape in the 1950's when I was a small child. They began as bedtime tales featuring Paul and his friends, myself and my sister Sheenagh, not forgetting the very real Ginger Odd Eyes. Yes, he really did exist, basking most of the time in the warmth of the greenhouse. These stories related to me by my mother sent me happily to sleep night after night.

Later Mum put pen to paper and created *The Adventures of Paul Sparrow*. Recently I discovered the manuscript, which had become dog-eared and tattered. For a number of years the family had talked about getting suitable illustrations and publishing the story, but up until now no one had created any drawn characters for the book. In 1991 my three sons aged thirteen, ten and eight decided they would like to tackle the task for their Nanny, and so we began.

I would like to give my thanks here to Fiona Daughton and John Staplehurst who typeset and published an earlier edition of the book, and to my three children Daniel, Adam and Peter for their illustrations.

It is now 2005, and the boys are grown. Added here are thanks to Stacey Matten for reformatting the book, and with love to Mum, now 91 years of age

Mary Collins
July 2005

Chapter 1

PAUL FINDS A NEW HOME

The trouble with Paul Sparrow was that he had never been very strong. From the moment his mother had pushed him with his brothers and sisters from the nest, he knew this. Quickly the others spread their wings and learnt to fly, but not poor Paul. His body felt too heavy for his weak wings to carry.

Fortunately, he managed to drift with the wind onto a rooftop, and a very lucky thing too, for down below in the garden sat Ginger Odd Eyes licking his paws and washing his face.

To cat lovers Ginger Odd Eyes was a very nice cat. He had one blue eye and one yellow eye, and this got him just that extra bit of attention that cats love.

Birds and mice did not think Ginger Odd Eyes was a nice cat, and Paul Sparrow felt the same. Paul tried once more to fly, keeping over the roof in case his wings failed him. His flying was still very weak, and he began to feel cold. He could not fly back to his Mummy's nest. He could not reach the trees. What could he do?

Just then he came to the chimney pot, and over this chimney pot was a dear little slate roof. This little roof was meant to stop the wind blowing down the chimney, but to Paul it was a haven, somewhere to rest out of the cold. To his great joy he found the chimney pot was warm, so he cuddled down to spend the night in this cosy place.

The next morning Paul felt much stronger. He walked along the rooftop and made a promise to practice flying later on. He saw two little girls playing in the garden and soon discovered that one was called Sheenagh and the other Mary Rose. Suddenly, to his great alarm, he saw Ginger Odd Eyes streak up through the garden. At the same time a bird flew into the air just in time to escape the clawing paws of Odd Eyes.

Then he heard the two little girls calling. "Ginger, you naughty cat, leave the birds alone!"

Paul found a funny feeling creeping into him, and he knew it was love for these two little girls that filled his tiny breast. Right then he decided to make his home in the cosy chimney pot house of this garden.

Later, while Ginger was asleep on the shelf in the greenhouse, Paul tried out his wings and found he could reach the garden very well. He hastily ate the crumbs that had been shaken from the table-cloth, and flew up again to the safety of the roof.

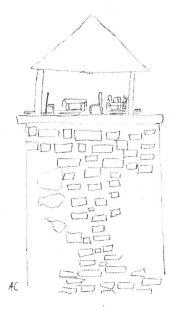

He looked around the garden. Yes, there should be good worm hunting here, he decided. The rain gutters would provide him with water to drink and for his daily bath. The trees looked green and fresh in the churchyard next door. Somewhere amongst them was his Mother's nest, and no doubt his brothers and sisters were making nests of their own. Paul felt just a little sad, and hopped slowly back to his own house. The central heating was fine, but the house did look a trifle bare.

Then he heard voices. "Let's make some chairs and tables from the cornflakes box, shall we Sheenagh?"

"Oh alright. You find the scissors and I'll ask Mummy for some Sellotape."

This will be interesting, thought Paul, his little head going from side to side and his tail flicking with joy. A little later he saw a neat little table, two chairs and a settee taking shape.

They were just finished when a bell suddenly rang and a grown up's voice said, "Pat says can you come over and play with her?"

The girls dashed off in four seconds, leaving behind their tiny furniture.

Now just guess what Paul began to think? Guess what he began to want? Yes, you are absolutely right! He thought the furniture would fit in his little house very well. It would look so like the room he could just see from the roof—a room with a table and chairs where the family had their meals.

He flew down to the garden and held a chair in his beak, but he could not manage to fly up again with it; he simply wasn't strong enough. He tried again and again; then, being only a baby bird, he began to cry. Big tears rolled down his beak and dropped in the yard. He hopped slowly away.

Suddenly a squeaky voice said, "Can I help you?"

Paul flew into the air chirping in alarm. He looked back and saw a sweet little mouse in a blue frock and tiny red apron.

"Don't be afraid," she said. "Ginger is not about. If he were I would not be here." She smiled. "Why are you crying?"

"Oh," said Paul in-between his sobs. "I have a dear little warm house to live in, and these chairs and this table would fit so well, but I can't get them up there."

"Where is this house?" asked the little mouse. Paul flew up and proudly pointed to his chimney pot house.

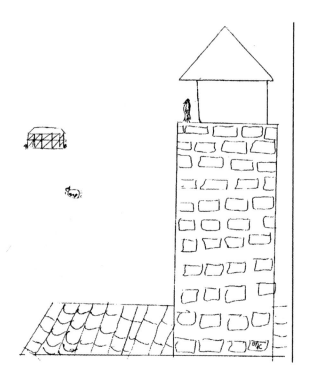

"I can get up there," said the mouse. "My name is Maggie. What are you called?"

"I'm Paul, and I am very glad to know you Maggie, but how can you reach my house? I find it rather hard, and at least I have wings, even if they are not very strong yet."

"I have secret passages all over the house," said Maggie. "I don't like living in a house where they keep a cat especially to frighten mice, but that's grown ups for you. They say we are a nuisance, yet only yesterday I saw Ginger Odd Eyes licking out the frying pan and helping himself to milk from the jug, and his saucer was half full of milk on the floor. I only have to nibble from the cheese and I hear the grown ups voice saying, 'Oh those horrid mice have been round again! I suppose Ginger was out all night.'"

"Why do you stay then?" asked Paul.

"Because luckily everybody in this house has not grown up yet. Mary Rose and Sheenagh love mice. They even have books with lovely mice pictures in them, and I have known them to fill their doll's plates with the most scrumptious odds and ends of food, and leave them right by my mouse hole. They have even called in and said, 'This is for you Maggie!' And I do enjoy it—unless a 'Grown up Tidy—upper' comes along."

Chapter 2

MAGGIE HAS A BUSY DAY

Paul awoke, stretched his wings and looked around. His eyes suddenly popped wide open—what was this? Could it be true? Yes, it must be.

There in his dear little house stood the sofa, two chairs and a really useful table. He hopped over to the sofa and just could not believe his eyes. On it was a really super cushion. It fitted the sofa completely, and on top of that was a lovely little tartan coverlet. He lay down on it. It was soft, and, strangely enough, very warm. He wondered where the warmth came from.

Then a voice said, "Do you like it?"

It was Maggie, hiding behind the sofa. She had been resting on it, waiting for Paul to wake up and had quickly hidden behind it when she saw him stretching. No wonder the cushion was still warm!

"Oh," said Paul, "it is perfect. Dear Maggie, how did you manage it all by yourself?"

"Through the secret passages right up to the roof rafters," said Maggie. "It was hard work but I love being busy. I heard a voice say, 'Whatever is that dragging noise? It must be mice behind the walls.'"

Paul looked around his house. There were the two chairs and the table, and on the table was a very pretty white cloth with lace around it.

"Where did you get the cloth?" asked Paul.

Maggie giggled. "I took it from a pile of ironing," she said. "It's really a ladies handkerchief. The plain ones make very good sheets and I keep my own home very well stocked that way."

Paul wondered if he should return the hanky, but Maggie said she was sure the people in the house would like Paul to have a pretty tablecloth, and that animals and birds were different to humans; most of them just have to help themselves where they can. Paul then flew off in search of food. He found some fine berries, a fair sized piece of currant cake, a portion of sausage roll and some potato peels from the hen's food. It took several journeys to get this to his house and as they had no plates Maggie said they must eat it on the floor to keep the tablecloth clean.

Later she hoped to get a few plates and cups from the toy cupboard. Maggie knew perfectly well that those dolls, Pandas, teddies and rabbits could not really eat and drink. Mary Rose was always giving them food on dainty little plates, and if Ginger Odd Eyes was not around Maggie usually scooped it into her own little larder. When they finished tea Maggie said she had work of her own to do and darted into the nearest secret passage.

Paul beamed. Yes, he really felt he was going to like it here with ready cooked meals on doll's tea plates. As for Ginger Odd Eyes, Paul had noticed one thing—cats certainly liked their sleep. There was that lazy Ginger fast asleep roasting in the sunshine!

"Goodbye Maggie," said Paul. "I am going for a little snooze myself."

"Goodbye Paul," said Maggie. "I'm no dormouse but I can do with a little nap." And off they both went for a nice little rest.

PC

Chapter 3

PAUL VISITS FOXY WOODS

Paul decided to fly a little further afield. He felt much stronger already. He soon came to a wood. Birds cheeped "Good day" to him and he flew down by a large tree trunk.

It seemed rather quiet, when suddenly a little voice said, "Oh botheration! If someone doesn't find me I shall be here all night." There was a pause and then the voice said, "I'll try calling for help. HELP! HELP! HELP!"

Paul was scared at first. He was still only a baby sparrow, but then he decided to be brave. He hopped about, his bright eyes darting here and there. Was that a red flower over there? He hopped over. It was a little gnome in a red jacket, green trousers and red hat. He had a beard and a cross face.

"I'm Brownie Big Toe. Just *look* what's happened to me!"

Paul looked down and saw that Brownie Big Toe had caught his big toe under a root of a tree. Try as he would he just could not get it free.

Paul tried to be helpful; he put his little beak under the root and tried to lift it with all his strength, but Brownie Big Toe gave a yell and said, "Stop digging me with your beak!"

"What can I do then?" said Paul.

"You had better find Dr. Knowalott," said Brownie.

"Where does he live?" asked Paul.

"At Clevernob in Foxglove Dell, Foxywoods."

Paul did not even know he was in Foxywoods and had no idea where to find 'Clevernob'. He could but try. He flew low, for pixies live low in the woods. It was then he met Roy Robin.

Roy had on a postman hat and a little mailbag hung from his neck.

"Excuse me," said Paul politely, "could you tell me where Clevernob house could be found?"

"Who be needing Dr. Knowalott then? What's 'appened?" asked Roy, who was a country robin.

"It's Brownie Big Toe," said Paul. "He has his toe caught in the root of a tree."

"Gaw, 'as he run into trouble with that toe again?" asked Roy.

"Oh please," said Paul, "do tell me where the doctor lives. Brownie was cross enough when I left him."

"Right, follow me," said Roy, and he swiftly flew into a soft grassy dell and stopped by a big tree. In the trunk of the tree was a little door, and on the door was carved 'I. Knowalott H.F.M.EX'.

"What do all the letters mean?" asked Paul.

"You do be ignorant," said Roy. "Them letters do mean High Fees, Medicine Extra."

Paul rang the bell. Soon the door opened and there stood a remarkable gnome. He had pinstriped trousers and a black coat, pince-nez spectacles, and a stethoscope hung from his neck.

"Come right in," he said to Paul. "Tell me what's wrong with you, and I'll tell you what not to do."

"Oh no! It's not me, it's Brownie Big Toe." "What's happened this time?" asked the doctor.

"His toe is caught under the root of a tree. Do come at once! He is getting so cross."

Dr. Knowalott bustled inside then returned with a case. He went round to the other side of the tree where there was another door, opened it, and there was a lovely little car.

"Lead the way!" he called, and away went Paul to where he had left Brownie Big Toe. Dr. Knowalott jumped out of his car and examined the toe. Then he opened his little case, took out some ointment and began to rub it into the root of the tree.

"It's not the tree that's sore, it's my toe!" screamed Brownie Big Toe, but Dr. K. continued to rub in the ointment and then rubbed it on the toe also. It melted and oozed all around the toe and the tree root.

"Now Pull, Pull, Pull!" he shouted.

Brownie Big Toe gave a big tug and his toe slid out from under the tree root.

"Just a minute," said the doctor and he took some clean cotton wool and scrubbed off all the grease. "If I leave that on he will be sliding his toe under another root before he gets home."

"Thank you so very much," said Brownie Big Toe "How much do I owe you?"

B.B.T. was a tailor by trade. The doctor considered.

"That will be one new waistcoat, and of course the ointment is extra—one pair of spats also please."

The reason Dr. Knowalott was the best-dressed gnome in Foxy-woods was that poor Tailor Brownie had such a very big toe, and had so many fees to pay.

Paul flew home. He felt tired and he wanted to tell Maggie all that had happened. She was very pleased for she did not know much of what went on elsewhere. She was a house mouse and did not care to venture far afield.

Chapter 4

LOPPY LOU FROM AUSTRALIA

Much as Paul loved chimney pot house, and the garden and exploring Maggie's secret passages, Foxywoods strongly attracted him. He loved to go there often to see his old friends and make new ones. To get to Foxywoods he had to cross the river. At first he flew over the bridge in case he needed a rest, but now his wing was so strong after a daily application of Dr. Know-alott's embrocation that he could fly to Foxywoods in a very short space of time, chirping to the swans as he passed over the river.

One day, when he was about to cross the river, he thought he heard the sound of crying. He looked around and there on the river bank he saw a sobbing rabbit. Paul had a kind little heart and he flew down at once.

"What's the matter?" he asked.

"I can't get to the woods," cried the little rabbit.

"Why don't you go back the way you came?" suggested Paul.

"If I did that I should go back to Australia," said the rabbit.

"Good gracious!" said Paul, "have you come all that way?"

"Yes, on a fine boat. I was a stowaway, but I got out of the boat on the wrong side of the river and I can't swim across to the woods."

Paul saw the problem immediately. There was only a mud bank here and rabbit must move before the tide came in.

"Stay here," said Paul, "I will fly up river and find my friend Sylvia Swan. If she is in a good temper and has had plenty to eat, I think she will ferry you across."

While Paul was away, rabbit hid behind a washed up tree trunk. Then she heard children's voices.

"Let's feed the swans," said one child.

"They are further up river," said another.

Rabbit looked up and saw three children leaning over the wall. One was almost a baby. There was a plop, and something fell in the mud. Then a baby voice began to yell.

"I've dropped my bag of crusts."

"You silly little thing," said the older children. "Never mind, we will go further up the river and you can share our crusts," and away they went.

Rabbit scooped up the bag of crusts. How lucky she felt, for these would make an excellent gift for Sylvia Swan. Shortly afterwards a graceful swan sailed smoothly down the river, Paul flying just ahead to show the way.

"How do you do?" said Sylvia graciously bowing here long neck. "I hear you are stranded; most unfortunate, but I am afraid you will have to wait a little longer. I am hungry and I feel sure some humans will be along soon with some scraps of food."

Rabbit held out the bag of crusts. "I saved these for you," she said.

Sylvia completely forgot her dignity and gracious airs. Her neck lunged forward in one swift movement and she grabbed the bag, emptied it into the water and gobbled them up swiftly before the gulls could rob her.

When not a single crust remained she smiled sweetly, politely thanked rabbit and once more assumed a queenly air.

"Hop on my back, I will now take you across the river."

Rabbit felt much happier when they arrived at the other side. She could see the lovely woods and they gave her a feeling of safety.

"Thank you so much for bringing me," she said to Sylvia.

"Oh, any time you wish to cross I shall be pleased to take you," said Sylvia. "Just send Paul to find me, and do tell me, what is your name?"

"I am Loppy Lou. I come from Australia."

"How very interesting. We must meet again. Goodbye for now."

Sylvia Swan glided away in stately style, Loppy Lou scuttled into the woods, and Paul flew low to keep her in sight.

"Stop here," called Paul. "This is 'Nutty House' where Sam and Sue Squirrel live. Perhaps they will put you up for a few days."

Mrs Squirrel answered the knock on the door.

"I'm so sorry," she said when she heard the request, "I have a houseful of visitors from Tall Forest. Why don't you try Barbara Bobtail? The twins will show you where she lives."

Sam and Sue led the way. Miss B. Bobtail lived in a very neat burrow under a hollow tree. On the tree was carved very simply B.B.B. which meant Barbara Bobtail's Burrow. The twins rang the bell. They chattered excitedly when Miss Barbara appeared, explaining where Loppy Lou had come from.

"Do come in," said Miss Barbara. "You must be tired and hungry."

She made an excellent cup of tea, produced some carrots and lettuce and, when Loppy Lou could not eat another morsel, she took her to her spare bedroom and settled her down for a good night's rest.

Paul was very pleased. He said goodnight to Miss Barbara and asked permission to call next day.

"Certainly," said Miss Barbara, "it was most kind of you to take so much trouble to get Loppy Lou safely to the woods."

Paul returned to his own little house. How lovely it was to have a home. Maggie was waiting to hear his latest adventure.

"Oh Paul, how lucky you are to be able to go about so much. Sometimes I wish I was a field mouse instead of a stay-at-home house mouse, but how lucky I am to have you to tell me everything that goes on."

Chapter 5

MAGGIE MOUSE GETS POORLY

One drizzly, rainy morning Paul awakened and peeped from behind his little curtain. It did look dreary. He would get some breakfast and wait for Maggie to come. He watched until he saw the breakfast cloth being shaken, made sure that Ginger Odd Eyes was not hiding in the doorway, swooped down and ate the smaller crumbs. One large piece of bread with butter on he took up to his house. Still he waited. Maggie did not come. Paul began to feel worried; Maggie could be tired today or she was too busy to come. Soon Paul got so lonely he decided to venture into the secret passages.

Until now he had only been through them with Maggie to show him the way. It was rather dark. Paul hopped along the rafters trying to remember which little hole Maggie usually went in. It must be this one.

After a while Paul found himself in a cupboard. He chirped, "Maggie, Maggie, Maggie," but found himself hopping in some soft black powder. Paul had never been here before. It must be the wrong place—there seemed to be some light further on.

Paul hopped towards it and he came out into daylight and found himself in a bedroom.

There were two beds—a short one and a long one. There were toys, a doll's cot, a doll's bed, teddies and pandas. Paul rightly decided that this was where Mary Rose and Sheenagh slept.

It was quiet—they must be at school. Once more Paul cheeped, "Maggie, Maggie, Maggie."

Suddenly things happened very quickly.

He heard a scurrying of padded paws, then Maggie's voice saying urgently, "Quick Paul, in here!"

He dived into a cupboard and Maggie quickly slammed the door just as Ginger Odd Eyes streaked into the room. What a fright they had had.

"I came to look for you, Maggie," said Paul.

"How brave of you, Paul. I'm so pleased to see you for I am feeling so very poorly."

"Oh Maggie, whatever is the matter?"

"I feel so cold and sick, I just want to stay in bed. Just press your beak on the light switch please."

Paul found the switch. The cupboard was quite big. It had shelves, books and more toys. On the lower shelf there were a number of small beds made from little cushions and lavender bags, from cardboard soap boxes and chocolate boxes, and from an old toy bath. Two were made from an old pair of slippers. All these beds were occupied by toys. There was Teddy Wee, and Wee Panda, Katie Kangaroo with her baby in a pouch, Martin Monkey who had come from the fair, Ferdi Faun and Cyril Squirrel. They had a variety of coverlets, mostly handkerchiefs and pretty pieces of material left over from the sewing box. Maggie got into one of the slipper beds.

"Is this where you usually sleep?" asked Paul.

"Oh no," said Maggie, "I came here because it is a hospital. I heard Mary Rose and Sheenagh say it was, and I don't feel so lonely with all these others around, although they cannot talk."

"I shall go at once to fetch Dr. Knowalott," said Paul.

"The window is open," said Maggie. "You need not use the secret passages. Just fly straight out of the window and come back that way. We must peep first and see if Odd Eyes has gone."

They carefully opened the door, which fortunately had a ball catch. Odd Eyes was not in sight. Paul swiftly flew out of the window and Maggie quickly shut the door of the cupboard.

Dr. Knowalott had just finished his surgery as Paul arrived.

"Can you come to see Maggie? She is not at all well."

"It's a very long way," said the doctor. "It would take me hours to get there in my car."

"If only I could carry you," said Paul, "but I am not strong enough."

"I shall have to buy a helicopter when I get rich. I find it hard enough to reach patients who live in the high trees."

"Caw! Caw! Caw!" screamed through the air. Paul was startled. He looked around anxiously and saw a huge rook swoop down beside him.

"Caw! Caw! Do you want transport? Caw! Caw! Where do you want to go?"

"Good morning Sir," said Dr. Knowalott, "and who may you be?"

"I am Reggie Rook. I will take you anywhere high or low. I will take you at any time in any weather for a reasonable fee."

"Very well, I am about to visit a sick housemouse. Follow Paul Sparrow," said Dr. Knowalott.

Maggie looked so pleased when they arrived in so short a time. Dr. Knowalott was so interested in the pretend hospital that he forgot at first to examine Maggie. He put his little stethoscope on her chest, tapped his finger on her back and tummy and then asked Maggie to put out her tongue.

"No, that's rude!" said Maggie.

"But I only want to see if it is furry," said Dr. Knowalott.

"Don't be ridiculous, it's the only part of me that isn't furry," said Maggie.

Dr. Knowalott looked cross.

Paul said, "Please Maggie, let him see your tongue. He really is clever."

Maggie opened her mouth wide. Dr. Knowalott peered in.

"Just as I thought. A sore throat—tonsillitis. You won't need much to eat, but plenty to drink instead. I will send you some medicine by Reggie Rook."

When they had gone, Paul picked up a small doll's beaker. He filled it with water from the bathroom and took it to Maggie. He stayed for a while until Reggie Rook returned with some sore throat tablets and a bottle of medicine.

Maggie soon fell fast asleep, for there was something in the medicine to help her to sleep soundly. Paul tucked in the bed-clothes, then flew out of the window to go on a worm hunt.

Maggie slept far too soundly. When she woke up she heard Mary Rose shouting excitedly to Sheenagh,

"Come and see what we have got in our hospital, Sheenagh. Quick! It's real! It's alive!"

Maggie knew exactly what she should do. In 10 seconds she should be through that hole through which the gas pipes came, but she could not move. She was drowsy, still poorly and firmly tucked in. She lay terrified. Would a grown up come upstairs, she wondered? Sheenagh ran into the room.

"What have you found, Mary Rose? What's alive?" Then she saw. "Oh what a dear little thing."

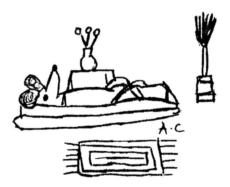

Mary Rose gently picked her up.

"Why did you come to our hospital little mouse? Are you poorly?" asked Mary Rose. Maggie trembled a little. "I'll put her back to bed. I hope she stays here."

Maggie was pleased to be back in the warm slipper bed. She heard Mary Rose say she would go downstairs and get food for all the children.

"Don't forget to shut the door so that Ginger can't get in our cupboard," said Sheenagh.

The children brought up food and water and a tiny vase of flowers. They put the food on the top of each little bed and did not forget Maggie.

"You can sleep in here as long as you like, dear little mouse," they told her, and when the door was firmly closed, she felt safe in doing so.

The next morning Maggie Mouse awakened feeling much better. She had slept off her drowsiness, her throat felt better and she had a good appetite. There was food everywhere. Every little toy animal had a plate with a tasty morsel on it. Maggie made a good many journeys to her own little home taking all the food with her.

"Perhaps the children will think the toys came alive at night by magic and ate the food," thought Maggie, but they did not. When they opened the cupboard in the morning they were sorry to find the little mouse had vanished.

They said, "She must have taken all the food with her. It will last her a long time." But it did not. Can you guess why? She sent Paul with most of it to Dr. Knowalott for his fee and to pay for the medicine. Dr. Knowalott secretly hoped that Paul would catch the sore throat, for he particularly liked the piece of blackberry and apple pudding which made part of his fee. Reggie Rook tried hard to get it as transport payment, but had to be content with a piece of dry sponge cake.

Chapter 6

THE WOODLAND PARTY

The days were getting colder and shorter and the trees were fast losing their leaves. Paul Sparrow was glad to have a warm snug home. He loved the lights all shining in the house. He knew exactly when Mary Rose went to bed for he saw the light in the children's bedroom and the bathroom. When the lights went out he knew that Mary Rose would soon be fast asleep, for she was the youngest in the house and the first to go to bed. When Mary Rose was asleep, Paul liked to snuggle down and go to sleep himself.

As the days were short, Paul made the most of them. Maggie was too busy a mouse to give Paul a lot of company and the woods had a natural attraction for him. One day when it was crisp and dry he flew into Foxywoods.

"Good morning Paul," said a quiet voice.

"Hullo Loppy Lou," said Paul. "I was hoping to see someone. How are you?"

"I like it here," said Loppy Lou. "Everyone is so friendly, but soon the days will be dark and cold and most of the animals will go to sleep."

"Oh dear," said Paul.

"I shall be lonely then. I shall miss you all."

"Wouldn't it be fun," said Loppy Lou, "if we could have a party?"

"Where could we have a really big party?" asked Paul. "Most of you have such small houses."

"We could have it in the wood on a lovely day like this," said Loppy Lou.

"Why not today?" asked Paul. "It may be raining on other days."

"We could try," said Loppy Lou. "We could ask all our friends to bring some-thing to a clear patch in the middle of Foxywoods."

"That's a good idea," said Paul. "If we lit a fire and cooked some food around it we could call it a barbecue. Humans often do that; we even had one in our back garden."

Paul and Loppy Lou decided to round up as many friends as they could find. Paul soon met Roy Robin the postman. Roy was somewhat annoyed when he heard about the party. He said it would be better if they had written invitations and given them to Roy to post.

Paul thought of a good idea.

He said he would write one letter, give it to Roy and ask him to let all the woodland folk read the same letter. In the letter he asked them all to bring what they could manage to the barbecue.

Early that afternoon they began to gather in the wood. Sue and Sam Squirrel, Miss B. Bobtail, Brownie Big Toe with his friend Brownie Bang-Bang the carpenter, and Bang-Bang's two apprentices Bzz Bzz and Saw Saw.

Dr. Knowalott came in his little car. Paul asked him if Reggie Rook was coming, but Dr. Knowalott just smiled and said, "Wait and see."

Many other small animals came bringing friends and relations, and they all brought something to eat—honey and nut cakes, blackberries, hips and haws. The birds brought worms and grubs and a few crusts. Sylvia Swan arrived. She looked as dignified as ever. She graciously apologised for bringing no food. In fact, she had started her journey with a few crusts, but she gobbled them up on the journey. Dr. Knowalott brought his bag with some tummy ache mixture in it in case anyone ate too much.

The fire was crackling merrily and it seemed as if everyone was there when suddenly "Caw! Caw! Caw!'" was heard by every-one. Reggie Rook was carrying an enormous load. Two baskets, one firmly held in each claw, and on his back a bundle. Tightly clutching the bundle, was—guess who? Just who do you think he was carrying?

Yes, it was little Maggie Mouse on her very first visit to Foxy-woods.

Dr. Knowalott came fussing up. He peered eagerly into the baskets. And what did he see? Sausage rolls, sandwiches, cakes, chocolate biscuits, meat and sausages to roast over the fire, and potatoes to bake. In the bundle was a big pudding, tasty little scraps of all sorts of things rolled together like a Christmas pudding.

Now the party really began. Sylvia Swan came over to chat with Maggie. She wondered where so tiny a mouse could get so much food. Maggie told her about the house she lived in and how the children looked after herself and Paul. She said she had a big surprise when Reggie Rook had called for her. It was really Dr. Knowalott's idea.

When they had eaten all the food, they sang songs and danced. Everyone was happy until a yell was heard, then everyone was quiet.

"It's Brownie Big Toe again!" someone cried, and sure enough, there he was with his big toe once more caught under a tree root. They heaved and pulled, but could not free the big toe. Dr. Knowalott came forward looking really important. He rubbed on his greasy ointment, but still the toe remained trapped. Poor Brownie Big Toe looked so unhappy. The ointment had worked last time. Dr. Knowalott now looked unhappy too; he had been hoping to earn a good fee for he fancied a new suit. Then Brownie Bang-Bang said he would like to try to release his friend. He got his little hammer and tried to knock the tree root away, but he only wedged it tighter and poor Big Toe was terrified he might get a bang from the hammer.

Suddenly the two little apprentice gnomes came running up. They had been home to get their own little tools. Each had a tiny saw. One got on either side of the big red toe, and there was a steady sound of *bzz bzz bzz* and *saw saw saw* as they sawed right through the tree root.

Big Toe was so pleased to be released that he promised the little pixie boys a brand new carpenter's apron each with lots of pockets for their tools.

They all went home tired and happy. Reggie Rook took Maggie only part of the way, for Sylvia Swan insisted on carrying her through the wood and to the other side of the river. Reggie was waiting to take her the rest of the way. She promised to send some food to Sylvia Swan occasionally, and promised Reggie Rook a good meal if he would carry it.

Maggie went to bed feeling so happy at having made so many new friends. She blessed the day when Paul Sparrow had come to live at this house and made these friendships possible.

The End

About the Author

Connie Haughton (nee Carey) was born on February 1st 1914 in Devon. From an early age she had a love for young children. She remembers her first job at the age of 16, which was in a crèche set up by Lady Astor (the M.P for Plymouth at the time). This was for the children of the local "fishwives". Later Connie became a nurse and she still fondly remembers many of the children she nursed.

Connie married Tom Haughton in 1936, and nursed in Plymouth during the war years. After the birth of her first child Paddy, Connie was recommended to take charge of a Nursery School in Plymouth run by the Astor Institute. Connie was able to take Paddy with her to work, and she remembers it as a very happy time. The children in the Nursery benefited from large amounts of story telling and opportunities to act out small plays and stories.

Later on Connie had Sheenagh, whilst the family were still living in Plymouth. In 1951 the family moved to Barnstaple where Connie's third child, Mary Rose, was born. The big house in Barnstaple is where the stories of Paul Sparrow began. One of the children was upset or frightened and Connie pointed out a little sparrow in the garden, which quickly distracted the little girl from her fears. From then on there was no turning back—the adventures of Paul Sparrow and his friends had begun. These stories developed as a way to distract Sheenagh and Mary Rose from their upsets. Connie quickly recognised that Paul's influence was like "magic" in the family, so the stories grew and became bedtime stories. Those in this volume are just a few which have been written down; many more exist within the Author's imagination.

Connie is now 91 years of age and has 14 grandchildren and 18 great-grandchildren.

More information at www.diadembooks.com/sparrow.htm

Mary Rose, Connie (the Author)
and Sheenagh

Mary Rose, Connie (the Author)
and Sheenagh

978-0-595-38147-(

0-595-38147-2

Printed in the United Kingdom
by Lightning Source UK Ltd.
107945UKS00001B/205-231